POLLY GREENBERG

illustrated by ALIKI

Oh Lord, I wish I was a buzzard

SeaStar Books   New York

Based on an experience told by Gladys Henton

Text © 1968 by Polly Greenberg
Revised text © 2002 by Polly Greenberg
Illustrations © 1968 by Aliki Brandenberg

First published in 1968 by Macmillan Publishing Co., Inc., New York.

SEASTAR BOOKS
A division of NORTH-SOUTH BOOKS INC.

Published in the United States in 2002 by SeaStar Books, a division of North-South Books Inc., New York. Published simultaneously in Great Britain, Canada, Australia, and New Zealand by North-South Books, an imprint of Nord-Süd Verlag AG, Gossau Zürich, Switzerland.
First SeaStar Books paperback edition published in 2003.

Library of Congress Cataloging-in-Publication Data
Greenberg, Polly.
Oh Lord, I wish I was a buzzard / Polly Greenberg; illustrated by Aliki.
p. cm.
Based on a childhood recollection of Gladys Henton of Greenville, Miss.
Summary: As a little girl picks cotton, she dreams of changing places with a buzzard, a dog, and other creatures of the field.
1. African Americans—Juvenile fiction. [1. African Americans—Fiction. 2. Cotton picking—Fiction.
3. Family life—Mississippi—Fiction. 4. Mississippi—Fiction.] I. Aliki, ill. II. Title.
PZ7.G8276 Oh 2002 2001049865
[E]—dc21

ISBN 1-58717-122-8 (trade edition)
10 9 8 7 6 5 4 3 2 1
ISBN 1-58717-123-6 (library edition)
10 9 8 7 6 5 4 3 2 1
ISBN 1-58717-220-8 (paperback edition)
10 9 8 7 6 5 4 3 2 1

Printed in Hong Kong

For more information about our books, and the authors and artists who create them, visit our web site: www.northsouth.com

To children all over the world
who work hard to help their families.

When I was a little girl,
we walked out to the cotton field
early in the morning
with the sun shining pretty on the land.

My Daddy told us
if we picked a lot of cotton
we might get a sucker.

We picked and we picked
and we picked and we picked.

It was hot, oh my, it was hot.
I looked up with the water running
off my face,
and I saw a dog lying under a bush,
going huh-huh-huh like dogs do.

I said, "Oh Lord, I wish I was a dog."

We picked and we picked
and we picked and we picked.

It was hot, oh my, it was hot.
I looked up with the water running
off my face,
and I saw a buzzard, going round and round
and round in the sky like buzzards do.

I said, "Oh Lord, I wish I was a buzzard."

We picked and we picked
and we picked and we picked.

It was hot, oh my, it was hot.
I looked up with the water running
off my face,
and I saw a snake, curved up cold and
cool near a rock like snakes do.

I said, "Oh Lord, I wish I was a snake."

We picked and we picked
and we picked and we picked.

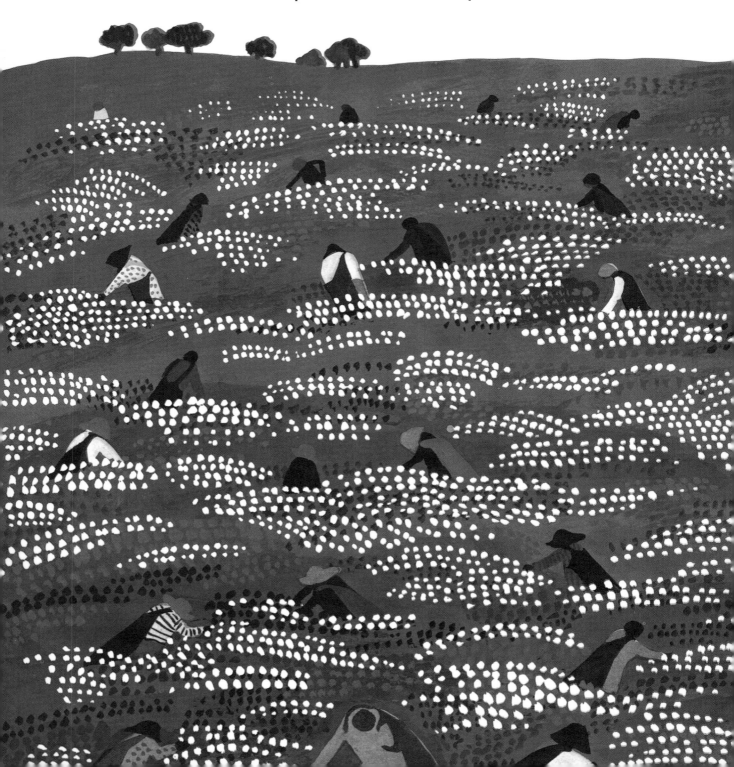

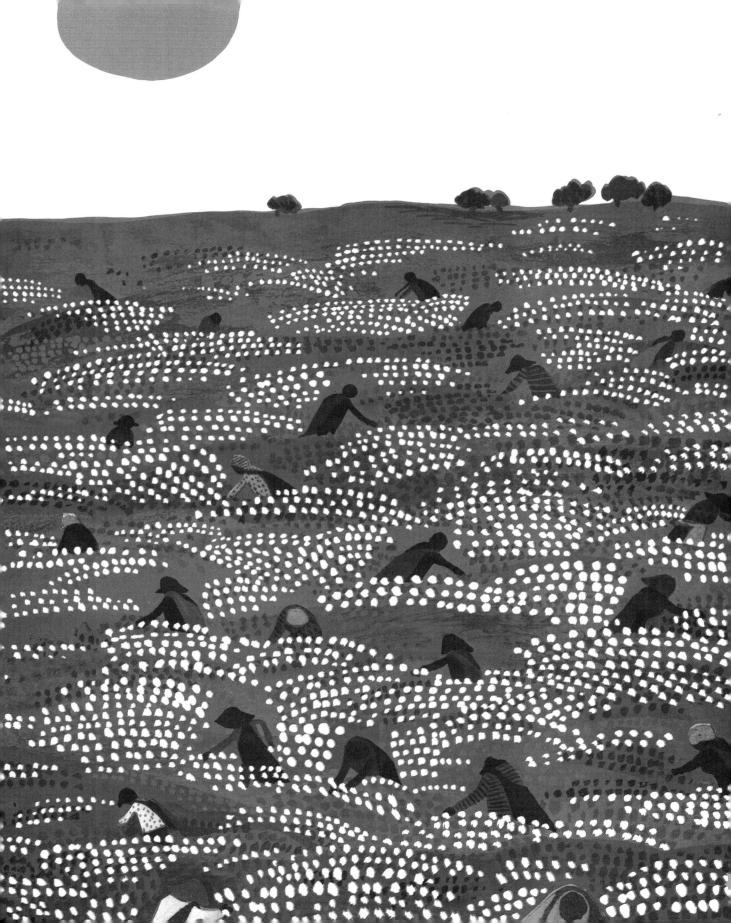

It was hot, oh my, it was hot.
I looked up with the water running
off my face,
and I saw a butterfly, bouncing from blossom
to blossom like butterflies do.

I said, "Oh Lord, I wish I was a butterfly."

We picked and we picked
and we picked and we picked.

It was hot, oh my, it was hot.
I looked up with the water running
off my face,
and I saw a partridge, circling
and clattering like partridges do.

I said, "Oh Lord, I wish I was a partridge."

When we were finished, on Saturday,
our Daddy gave us our suckers.
Mine was red.

I put the candy in my hand and the
stick in my mouth so all the kids
could see we had candy, lots of candy.
We licked and we licked
and we licked and we licked.

We walked home from the cotton field,
late in the evening,
with the moon shining pretty on the land.

FROM THE CHILDREN OF THE MISSISSIPPI DELTA TO CHILDREN EVERYWHERE . . .

In the project widely known as CDGM (Child Development Group of Mississippi), parents, sharecroppers, and other concerned residents of this vast rural area organized committees to act as school boards, found and fixed buildings, and hired people (most of them mothers of Head Start children) to teach and to run 120 centers for 12,000 children. The project provided paychecks and learning opportunities for 1,100 extremely low-income people.

It was from this group that the goals of CDGM emerged. Since the literature available for children at the time was extremely foreign to the boys and girls in this group, the few early childhood educators and consultants involved encouraged those working in the centers to recall their own real-life everyday occurrences from childhood and tell them as stories that would delight children and bring their culture into the classroom. Some of these anecdotes were written down word for word—as were many of the children's experiences. They were duplicated, made into homemade books, and given to each child as learning-to-read material. They were books of their very own to take home.

The story in this book is based on a childhood recollection told by Gladys Henton of Greenville, Mississippi, now deceased. In the 1960s, when this book was first published, she was amazed and excited that a simple oral narrative could be transformed into a real book, so that children of all regions—north, south, east, and west—could share in her experience.

NOTE TO FAMILIES AND TEACHERS

There are still a great many children in the world who work very hard to help their families. Before the U.S. child labor law was passed in 1935, large numbers of children of all races in the United States worked as many as fourteen hours a day in factories and other places of employment. Young readers should understand that this story took place before their grandmothers were born. Have a discussion with them about what they do to help their families today. Ask them to describe what they might want to do when they grow up, and to share ideas about what Gladys Henton, the girl in this book, may have done when she became an adult. Through conversations like these, children begin thinking about the inevitability of change and about the need for choice.

Gladys Henton grew up during a time when the majority of African-Americans had very few choices. While adults today realize that Caucasians are rarely as wealthy as they may appear in television shows and that most African-Americans do not work in cotton fields, children gather knowledge through what they experience, directly or through books and other media. In order to avoid instilling stereotypes, we need to share as many books as possible about all peoples of color from all walks of life. Fortunately, there are many good ones available; a children's librarian or the Children's Book Council (www.cbcbooks.org) can help you find them.

—Polly Greenberg